COMING OF AGE

THE DAY OF SELF PLEASURE

CLOVER'S FANTASY ADVENTURES
BOOK 13

VICTORIA RUSH

VOLUME 13

CLOVER'S FANTASY ADVENTURES -
BOOK 13

COPYRIGHT

For the uninhibited...

1

———

After their exciting adventure at the Sannyan temple, Clover and her friends took a well-deserved break to feast on wild boar and roasted rabbits before falling into a long, deep slumber. Upon recovering their strength the next day, they continued on their way, with no particular plan or destination in mind.

Their travels had taken them thousands of miles, from the northern reaches of Abbynthia to the sub-tropical rainforest of Sotharius. Although their itinerant wanderings had led them into the occasional tight spot, they were confident that their unique combination of skills and experience would protect them from whatever surprises lay around the next corner.

"So where to now?" Clover said, placing her hand over her brow as she peered at the rising sun coming up from the East.

"Not further south, that's for sure," Jessop said, pulling his sticky shirt away from his clammy skin. "I'm already sweating in this humidity this early in the morning."

"Why don't we head into the mountains to get a better

view of the surrounding terrain?" Tara said, pointing toward a tall ridge a few miles in the distance. "At the very least, we might be able to find some sheep and elk to mix up our diet."

"Some roasted lamb chops sounds delicious," Jessop nodded.

"Sounds good to me," Clover said, packing up her belongings and hoisting them over her back. "Shall I take the point position?"

"That makes the most sense," Tara said. "You're the least threatening, in case we run into some belligerent natives. We don't want a repeat of our nasty experience at the witches' coven."

Clover turned to face Tara and placed her hands on her hips, furrowing her brow in displeasure.

"Are you saying I don't pull enough of my weight around here?" she said.

"No," Tara chuckled. "It's just because you're the prettiest. You're the least likely to be speared at first sight."

"Hmph!" Clover huffed, not sure if Tara's comeback was an insult or a compliment.

"I'll take up the rear to protect our six," Jessop said, strapping his long cutlass onto the side of his hip.

"Who are you kidding?" Tara said. "You just want to be in the ideal position to stare at our jiggling butts while we traipse through the bush ahead of you."

"I'll admit that doesn't hurt," Jessop smiled, slapping his friend's ass playfully. "But you're in the best position, being in the middle with your expert archery skills if we detect any danger on our flanks."

"Alright," Tara said. "Let's not waste all day arguing over the arrangement of our marching formation. We should try to get to the top of those mountains before the sun drains all of our energy."

The trio headed into the brush, with Clover keeping a sharp eye out for any sign of movement while Tara kept one hand on the bow slung over her shoulder and Jessop tried his best to keep his eyes from wandering back to his friend's bouncing asses. Even though they'd just enjoyed in an orgy of sensual delights at the erotic temple, his libido was quickly returning, and he could feel his swelling tool rubbing against the insides of his tight pants every time he stepped over a fallen tree branch.

By midday, they'd already captured and skinned two bighorn sheep and a mountain goat, cooking and drying up the leftover meat as jerky for extra provisions. When they crested the top of the mountain, they peered out at the verdant valley stretching out for miles in every direction. The scene looked like something out of a fairy tale book, with lush jungle teeming with flitting birds and the screech of monkeys echoing above the tall canopy.

"I don't imagine there'll be much of a market for these pelts down there," Jessop frowned, cinching his heavy bundle of animal furs higher up on his back.

"I dunno," Tara said, scanning the luxuriant landscape for any sign of human habitation. "It can still get pretty cool at night. At the very least, they should make for warm bedcovers."

"It looks like there's some kind of settlement in that direction," Clover said, pointing her finger toward a clearing next to a large river where a thin tendril of smoke rose lazily over the treetops.

"Yes," Tara said, squinting at a circular formation in the middle of the camp. "It seems that they've taken the time to build up some fortifications. They might have some food or other resources we can trade for our pelts."

"Let's hope their walls aren't as tall as those at the land of giants," Clover said, wrinkling her forehead. "We got into a bit of a pinch trying to get out of that one."

"Maybe it's another kind of temple like the one we saw with the Sannyans," Jessop said, raising his brows hopefully. "Where they sacrifice their maidens for the approval of their gods."

"Do you ever think of anything besides sex?" Tara huffed, shaking her head at Jessop's one-track mind.

"You have to admit, it's been a while," he smiled. "I can't stop reliving some those insane hookups we had with those statues that came to life."

"I'm pretty sure that was a one-off," Clover chuckled, noticing the snake bulging down the side of Jessop's trousers. "Once their deity exploded, everybody disappeared into the ether."

"Who's to say some of them didn't make it out here?" Jessop said.

"It's worth an investigation," Tara nodded. "Just be sure to keep your wits about you and your dick in your pants until we discover if this new group is friendly or not."

"Not to worry," Jessop grinned, patting his long sword dangling from the side of his hip. "My weapon is well holstered."

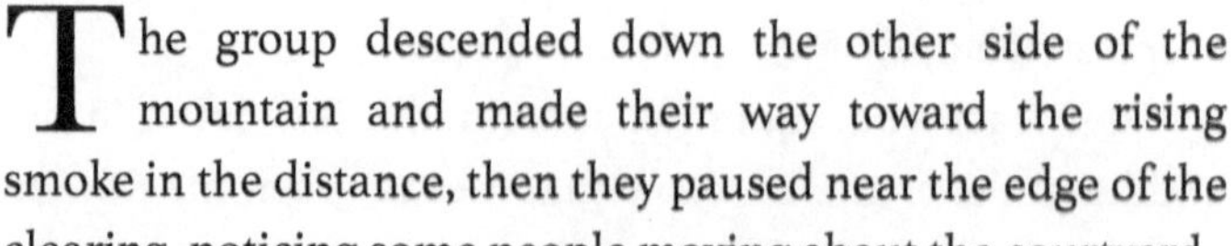

The group descended down the other side of the mountain and made their way toward the rising smoke in the distance, then they paused near the edge of the clearing, noticing some people moving about the courtyard.

"Are you seeing what I'm seeing?" Jessop said to his friends, widening his eyes as he took in the scene.

"It's pretty hard to miss," Clover nodded while her pupils dilated in excitement.

"Settle down," Tara said, keeping one hand near her quiver of arrows. "Just because everyone's running around naked doesn't mean they're not still a threat."

"So much for trading our animal pelts," Jessop said. "It looks like these people don't have the need for any kind of clothing whatsoever."

"They don't look like much of a threat to me," Clover said. "At least the advantage of meeting people without any clothes means they don't have anywhere to hide their weapons."

"I agree," Jessop said. "Perhaps it's best to lay down our arms and approach them slowly to show we mean no harm."

"Maybe," Tara said, scanning the rest of the courtyard and noticing people of all ages strolling around naked as a jaybird. "But we should be careful. Stay close to the edge of the thicket in case we need to make a hasty escape back into the safety of the woods."

"Maybe we should take off our clothes, too?" Jessop smiled.

"That might not have the effect you intended," Clover chuckled, glancing at the detumescent genitals of the people prancing around the village. "With your dick standing at half staff, you're just as likely to scare them away as invite them into our embrace."

"There'll be plenty of opportunity for fraternizing later," Tara said. "Right now, our best chance is to show them we mean no harm."

"Why don't I go first?" Clover smiled. "Since I'm apparently the least threatening one..."

"Alright," Tara nodded. "You go ahead and introduce yourself while Jessop and I will wait under cover until you indicate the coast is clear."

"Okay," Clover said, unstrapping her bullwhip from beside her waist and laying it in the brush before rising up slowly from behind a bush.

She walked out tentatively onto the edge of the court-yard with her hands slightly elevated to indicate she came in peace, and some of the villagers froze when they saw her animal-skin leotard clinging to her nubile frame. One of the younger girls ran into an adjacent hut and emerged a few moments later with an older woman who was wearing a feathered headdress.

"Hello," Clover said as she slowly approached the elderly woman. "My name is Clover."

"What are you doing invading our peaceful settlement?" the woman said, peering at Clover with pinched eyebrows.

"I'm not invading," Clover said. "My friends and I were simply passing through when we came upon your village."

"How many of you are there?" the woman said, squinting behind Clover towards the edge of the thicket where she'd first emerged.

"There's only three of us. One man and two women."

"What is your purpose here?" the elderly woman said, placing her arm over the front of the younger girl's torso and moving her behind her body.

"We were hoping we could rest here for the night. And perhaps trade some of our trappings for things of equal value."

"What sort of trappings?"

"Mostly dried animal meat and pelts."

"We can always use more meat to feed our hungry mouths," the woman nodded. "As for the pelts–"

"Yes," Clover nodded, staring at the naked figures of the tribespeople assembling in a crowd behind the bare woman and child. "It would appear you don't have quite as much need for those..."

"On the contrary," the woman smiled. "We can put those to a special use. Tell your friends to reveal themselves."

Clover turned around and motioned to Tara and Jessop crouching at the edge of the thicket, nodding her head to indicate it was safe to come out.

As they stood up and began walking in the direction of the congregation, the old woman ran her eyes up and down their buff figures, nodding approvingly at their bulges in all the right places.

"Exactly how old are your friends?" she asked Clover.

"I'm not entirely sure," Clover said. "But I think they're roughly the same age as me."

"And how old are you?"

"Eighteen."

"In that case," the old woman smiled with a widening grin. "You're more that welcome to join us for as long as you want."

2

"Hello," Tara said to the elderly woman as she and Jessop approached the group. "My name is Tara, and this is Jessop."

"Pleased to meet you," the woman said, motioning to a steaming fire pit in the middle of a large amphitheater in the center of the courtyard. "My name is Gisella. Are you hungry from your travels?"

"We've eaten recently, thank you," Tara nodded. "In fact, we have extra food if you and your townsfolk would like to trade for some other provisions."

"We lead a pretty simple life here," the woman said. "What do you need?"

"Maybe some vegetables to round out our diet if you grow your own crops," Clover said, noticing some tilled fields on the side of the clearing.

"We'd be happy to share," the woman said, noticing Jessop ogling the naked figures of the young women clustered in a group behind her. "Were you looking for anything else?"

Jessop paused as he became increasingly conscious of the tightening feeling in his leggings.

"Do you mind our asking why your people choose to not wear any clothes?" he said.

"Well, for one thing," the woman said, noticing the prominent bulge in the front of his pants. "It can get pretty warm in the valley, and we find it more comfortable to allow our skin to breathe in the natural element. But more than that, we've always been an open community, with no desire to conceal our innate beauty or repress our natural instincts."

"Yes, I can see that," Jessop nodded as he soaked up the spectacle of the tribespeople's glistening, toned bodies. "Your people are very beautiful."

"As are each of you," Gisella said, darting her eyes over the figures of the three young travelers. "Perhaps you'd like to remove your own clothes and join our group for our mid-day feast?"

"Um—okay.," Clover hesitated, realizing the best way to acclimate with a new group was to adopt its customs. "Right here?"

"You can store your belongings in my cabin until you need them later," the woman nodded. "It's never too late to shed your inhibitions and share the natural beauty that Bestius bestowed upon all of us."

The trio paused for an awkward moment, then Jessop slowly began to unbuckle his belt.

"Right," he said, eager to free his swelling member pressing against his straining pants.

When he pulled his trousers down and his semi-erect prick swung up over his belly, he blushed.

"You'll have to excuse me, but I'm not used to being surrounded by so many beautiful naked women."

"Not to worry," the woman smiled, nodding at his impressive organ. "We welcome all forms of natural body expression."

Clover and Tara followed suit, and in short order, all of their clothes lay crumpled in a pile on the ground. The woman motioned for the young girl to gather their belongings and take them to her hut, then she invited the friends to join her in the large, circular amphitheater. As they walked toward the rest of the congregation, the crowd surrounded them, with the younger members of the group giggling and murmuring amongst themselves. When they reached the stadium, the old woman motioned for the trio to make themselves comfortable on the straw-mat-lined stone steps while she fetched three steaming bowls of chicken-vegetable soup.

"Thank you," Clover nodded when the woman passed each of the friends a bowl and the rest of the village took their places in the amphitheater to share the bounty.

"Mmm," Tara smiled, taking a sip of the delicious broth. "This is a welcome change from our usual diet of wild game and berries."

"Not to mention the unending sight of prickly pine trees," Jessop smiled, swiveling his head at the array of beautiful tribespeople arranged in a giant circle around them.

"This is quite an impressive structure you've built," Clover nodded, admiring the scale of the large grandstand built to accommodate hundreds of spectators. "Do you use this only for sharing your communal meals?"

"Actually," the woman said. "It was built for a very different purpose. We perform a ritual every night where this design provides the perfect viewing perspective."

"Oh?" Tara said, reflecting back on the unpleasant surprise awaiting their group when they stumbled upon the

BDSM dungeon of the witches' coven a few months previously.

Gisella nodded as she smiled demurely.

"As part of our desire to break down our young people's inhibitions regarding their sexual gifts, every person upon reaching the age of eighteen is expected to take this stage and stimulate themselves to orgasm in front of the entire village."

"What?" Tara said, spilling some of her soup over her thighs as she spewed her last mouthful back into her bowl. "Why not just let them learn and experience self-pleasure in the usual way? Most adolescents quickly learn how to satisfy themselves in the privacy of their own rooms–"

"True," the woman nodded. "But doing so in full view of the entire congregation has additional benefits. For one thing, everybody has a different way of pleasuring themselves, and seeing how each person does it gives the rest of us a chance to broaden our own sexual horizons. Plus, it acts as a natural aphrodisiac to perform such an intimate act in the presence of others. And there's one other benefit..."

"I can't imagine," Tara said, shaking her head in shock.

"Every month, on the emergence of the full moon, the two winners of the previous month's performances join up to perform a special paired union. It's a wonderful way to encourage continued creativity in our sexual practices and also enable our younger members to find suitable mates."

"How do you decide upon the winners?" Jessop said.

"All of the tribespeople vote at the end of the month for their favorite male and female performance, then the two individuals with the most tallies join together to demonstrate a special act of congress."

"Wow," Clover said, suddenly conscious of the moisture that had been building up between her legs while she listened to the old woman's description of the erotic ritual. "And there's a new performance every night?"

"Given the size of our community, there's usually a new person achieving the age of majority on any given day. We host the demonstrations most evenings at dusk on this very stage, illuminated by a circle of candles."

"And what do the rest of the viewers do while they watch?" Tara said, squirming uncomfortably as her own pussy twitched and pulsed, imagining the spectacle.

"We watch, of course, with intense interest, sometimes encouraging the performers to try different techniques. And often we stimulate ourselves at the same time, depending on how exciting we find each performance."

"Holy crap!" Jessop said, feeling his now hard-as-a-rock dick pressing up against his stomach as he imagined the many young tribal women jilling themselves in full view of the crowd. "That sounds incredibly exciting."

"So I can see," the woman smiled, glancing down at his bouncing erection. "Perhaps each of you would like to take a turn before you move on to the next step in your journey?"

"We'll be happy to watch at first," Clover chuckled. "Perhaps we can pick up a few pointers to expand our own repertoire of sexual tricks."

"I'm sure you will," the old lady smiled, noticing the puddle of fluid building up on the stone step in front of Clover's and Tara's pussies.

3

____

For the remainder of the day, Clover, Tara, and Jessop wandered about the village, introducing themselves to the different members of the group while exchanging gifts and provisions for different objects of interest. The old lady purchased all of their animal pelts, exchanging them for an unlimited supply of fruits and vegetables grown on their plantation. When the trio returned to their temporary quarters to prepare for the evening's demonstration, they placed their trinkets in a corner of the room, resting on the edge of the single oversize bed, shaking their heads in wonder.

"Can you believe our luck stumbling upon this over-sexed nudist camp?" Jessop said, staring at his friends with wide eyes. "I thought we'd died and gone to heaven when we discovered the erotic temple with statues of naked people who come to life. But this is a virtual cornucopia of erotic delights with everyone running around naked."

"Maybe so," Tara said. "But I think we should play it cool until we see how open and friendly these people really are.

We don't want to press our luck and intermingle too directly with the group until we know they're ready to welcome us into their full embrace. Especially with the younger members of the group, who seem to be required to save themselves until they're ready to present themselves to the public."

Clover paused as she nodded at Tara, deep in thought.

"They must get pretty worked up waiting to have open sex until they're eighteen," she said. "Especially watching their counterparts getting off every night in full view of the rest of the village."

"I imagine so," Tara said. "All the more reason to go hand's-off until we know they're ready."

"Speak for yourself," Jessop said, twisting the tip of his swelling organ between his fingers while his tool began to stiffen as he anticipated the spectacle of the upcoming performance later that evening. "There's nothing stopping me from indulging in a little of my own self-pleasure in the meantime."

"You might want to save that for later," Tara chuckled, watching him stroke his erection as it began to rise over his belly. "Something tells me you'll enjoy it a lot more with a little extra visual stimulation."

"I wonder if it will be a boy or a girl who performs tonight?" Clover said, rubbing her pussy unconsciously. "I have to agree with Jessop that this whole arrangement is a highly erotic setup. I can't wait to see what they do on stage in front of the whole group."

"Does it matter?" Tara said. "Either way, it's going to be an eye-opener and an interesting performance. Watching them alternate genders every night will give us plenty of ideas for expanding our own sexual experiences."

"Speaking of which," Jessop grinned, noticing his friends' inner thighs glistening from obvious arousal. "Why wait two hours until we can enjoy ourselves? It's been a while since any of us have had an orgasm. Why don't we have a little three-way to ease the tension before the big show?"

"He has a point," Clover nodded, turning to peer at Tara's swelling nipples. "What else are we going to do sitting alone in this empty cabin with one big bed? I've been wanting to touch myself ever since I saw all those pretty boys and girls lined up at the fire pit."

"I suppose it wouldn't hurt," Tara chuckled, staring at Jessop's big hard-on bouncing excitedly over his stomach. "What did you have in mind?"

"Well, since there's two girls and only one boy in this arrangement, why don't we do it Jessop's favorite way?" Clover said. "With the two of us tribbing each other in a crouched position while he sticks his dick between our two pussies."

"Okay," Tara grinned. "That's always pretty hot. It would be nice to take the edge off so I can enjoy the night's performance with our full concentration..."

"Assume the position then," Jessop smiled, stroking his dick while he contemplated fucking his two friends.

Clover flopped down on her back onto the bed, raising her spread knees up to her chest, then Tara squatted down overtop of her until their pussies mashed together, displaying their dripping vulvas and upturned asses for Jessop's consideration.

"Fuck, yes," he grunted, kneeling behind their glistening buttocks and sliding his throbbing tool between their two slits.

∼

The trio slept together on the oversize bed for a while, then they got up when they noticed the light beginning to dim in the courtyard, making their way to the amphitheater with the rest of the villagers. When they got to the stadium, the old lady was already waiting for them, motioning for them to take a front-row seat in the grandstand directly in front of the circular dais in the middle of the theater surrounded with a row of tall, flickering candles.

"Welcome," Gisella said when she saw the newcomers approaching. "I've saved a premium spot for your viewing pleasure as our special guests. I trust you found your new living arrangements comfortable?"

"Very," Clover smiled, winking toward her friends. "We've been eagerly looking forward to this evening's performance all afternoon."

"So I can see," the woman grinned, noticing the crusty residue from their afternoon interlude still coating the insides of their thighs and the top of their stomachs. "Come, sit together while we prepare for our new performer."

"Will it be a boy or a girl?" Jessop said, glancing at the nubile bodies of the young tribespeople as they took their places on the terraced steps surrounding the stage.

"A girl," the woman smiled. "Or perhaps I should I say a woman. This is her first presentation as an adult, and everyone is eager to demonstrate their appreciation to her as a fertile member of the community."

"Why not have them hookup as couples for their first sexual performance?" Tara squinted at Gisella. "If part of your goal is to showcase their reproductive abilities?"

"We believe everyone should be free to choose their own sexual partners, not forced to connect in an artificial coupling just to satisfy the prurient interests of our group."

"And yet you force at one couple to join together on this stage once a month at every full moon?" Clover said.

"Technically, they're not forced to do anything," the old woman said. "But we have yet to find a single couple who aren't willing to satisfy the rules of the game after the final votes are tallied."

"I bet," Jessop smiled. "They've got a whole month to imagine having sex with another person while they become increasingly worked up watching their peers stimulating themselves in ever-inventive ways for the benefit of the entire group."

Tara paused as she pondered just how far the tribe might take their novel approach to sexual entertainment.

"Do you ever match same-sex couples together?" she said. "That might be kind of interesting every now and then for a change of pace..."

"Not yet," the old lady said. "Although we're aware that members of our group enjoy the occasional lesbian and gay liaison, we like to encourage heterosexual hookups for their first couple experience to ensure the continued expansion of our community."

The three friends peered at one another as they pondered the old woman's comments.

"Do you ever engage in homosexual sex yourselves?" Gisella said.

"We've been known to experiment from time to time," Jessop grinned.

"Well, since there's two girls and only one boy in your group, perhaps you'd like to demonstrate some of your favorite techniques for us when you feel up to the task?"

"Perhaps," Tara said, noticing a young native girl approaching the rear of the stage. "Let's see how this plays out first. We don't want to rain on your parade, in a manner of speaking."

4

———

The three friends watched the naked girl ascend the steps at the back of the stage, then walk slowly toward the center of the raised platform. The flickering candles cast glimmering reflections on her beautiful figure, highlighting the natural curves of her firm breasts and her heart-shaped ass.

"She's beautiful," Clover gushed. "But why is she covering up her lower extremities with her hands?"

"Many of our new performers are a little shy when they first get on the stage. It takes a few moments for them to summon their courage and expose themselves fully for the group."

The assembled crowd watched the adolescent quietly for a few moments, then they began to clap softly, gradually raising the volume of their applause. The girl paused for a moment as she smiled demurely, then she slowly pulled her hands away from her crotch, revealing a small patch of pubic hair on the front of her mound.

"Are you sure she's eighteen?" Tara said. "She looks like she barely passed through puberty."

"Absolutely," the woman said. "We keep meticulous records of the time of month and year of birth of each of our citizens. No one is allowed to come out until they've full ripened, so to speak."

"She certainly looks ripe for the plucking," Jessop grunted, feeling a rush of fresh blood returning to his spent organ as it slowly began to swell. "That is, in terms of enjoying the pleasures of the flesh."

Clover tilted her body forward a few inches, squinting more closely at the stage.

"Those animal skins she's standing on look familiar," she said. "Are you using some of the ones we gave you earlier?"

"Yes," Gisella nodded. "The sheepskin hides in particular are super-plush and extremely soft. They're the perfect floor coverings for someone to lay their naked body."

"I'm glad we could help in some small way," Jessop chuckled while he watched the girl turn around, revealing her perfect tight ass and hourglass figure before reclining on the fluffy mats, face-down.

As the group continued to encourage her with gentle applause, she slid her arms under belly until her fingers emerged in the small space between her parted lips. The three friends could see the reflection of her moist pussy from the surrounding candles, and they gasped when they saw the girl's hands moving slowly over her darkened slit.

"She's not showing much so far," Jessop complained, eager to see the girl's sex revealed in all its glory while she stimulated herself.

"Give her some time to get in the mood," Gisella said. "It takes time for our newcomers to work up their courage and forget that a thousand eyes are watching them."

Clover slipped her hand between her thighs as she

watched the pretty girl stimulating herself, slowly beginning to finger herself.

"Personally, I think it's hot as fuck," she said. "Sometimes, less is more to get everyone in the mood. I could watch that perfect ass all night..."

"It is pretty sweet," Tara nodded, pinching her nipples softly as she gawked at the pretty tribesgirl. "Watching her flexing buttocks while she plays with her pussy is driving me crazy with anticipation."

"I'm sure she'll open up a little more as she becomes more aroused," Gisella said. "Everybody's inhibitions soon fall away once they feel their body acquiring a mind of its own."

"I know what you mean," Jessop huffed, twisting the tip of his swelling glans between his legs as his breathing began to become more ragged watching the girl writhing on the stage.

"Fuck me," Clover groaned, slipping two fingers into her dripping slit as she circled her clit with her other hand. "Now she's raising her hips a little higher and spreading her legs further apart..."

"I told you it was going to get more interesting," Gisella smiled, watching the three friends touching themselves while they stared at the sexy spectacle of the naked girl twisting her body in rising pleasure while the candlelight flickered over her flawless skin and body.

"Yes," Tara nodded, spreading her own legs slowly apart as she worked her glistening pussy with two hands. "I can see her glistening vulva and her parted lips clearly now. That is so hot."

"Jesus," Jessop grunted, grabbing his rock-hard dick with two hands while he stroked his erection with diminishing concern for the darting glances of the surrounding patrons who were busy stroking their own genitals while they watched the sexy girl on the stage. "How I'd love to sink my dick into that perfect ass..."

"You might get your chance if you play your cards right," the old lady said, widening her eyes at his swelling glans and his darkening shaft as Jessop squeezed his throbbing dick harder. "Although you might need to find some more inventive ways to stimulate yourself in public beyond the usual way."

"Oh, I've got plenty of other tricks in the bag," Jessop groaned, squeezing his testicles with his left hand while he jerked his shaft harder with his other hand.

"And what about you ladies?" Gisella said, turning to peer at Clover and Tara stroking themselves as they nestled one thigh over the other's shaking leg. "Have you got a few extra tricks in your bag?"

"You have no idea," Clover panted as she thrust the fingers of her right hand deep into her pussy, knuckle-deep.

"I'm pretty sure I've seen just about everything by now," Gisella chuckled while she rubbed her thighs together softly as she squirmed in unison with the rest of the spectators watching the girl moaning increasingly loud on the stage while she raised her ass higher in the air and her hips trembled on the precipice of climax.

"Maybe so," Tara panted, feeling her own orgasm beginning to well up deep in her belly. "But you haven't yet seen what two girls can do to one another when they set their mind to it."

"Not for a while perhaps," the old lady chuckled, starting to shake in her own rising pleasure. "I might not be as young as you or our pretty performer, but I still remember what it feels like to have sex with a woman."

Suddenly, the girl on the stage slipped two fingers into

her quivering hole as she rubbed the palm of her hand over her flaring bead. She paused as she felt her climax begin to wash over her, then she began shaking uncontrollably while she clenched her buttocks tightly and shook violently over the soft sheepskin rug. The three friends watched intently as a waterfall of fluid began to pour out of her pussy over her hands onto the plush rug.

"Oh my God," Jessop grunted, shooting a string of long ropes onto the floor of the theater while he gripped his purple phallus tightly in his hands. "That is crazy hot–"

"No shit," Clover gasped, jerking her body back and forth as she squirted her own juices between her thighs and over her clenching hands.

"Fuckkkk," Tara groaned in unison with her two friends while she rocked her hips, clasping her dripping pussy with two hands.

As the girl on the stage moaned and squealed in delirious rapture, a loud hum began to echo around the circular amphitheater as the rest of the crowd expressed their own peaking pleasure, watching the girl demonstrate her budding sexuality for the first time. When she finally stopped moaning and collapsed onto the soft animal skins with her glistening body shining in the reflection of the flickering candles, a soft applause began to spread from one one side of the auditorium to the other as people stood up and applauded the sexy performance of the pretty nymph. Jessop and the two friends rose out of their seats together with the old woman, nodding their heads in approval as they hooted and clapped with everybody else.

"Did you enjoy our little performance?" Gisella said, peering down at their dripping crotches and flushed chests.

"Very much so," Clover panted, still shaking from her powerful orgasm. "That's something I've never seen before."

"You mean watching a young woman stimulating herself?"

"I've seen that plenty of times," Clover nodded. "Just not surrounded by hundreds of naked spectators enjoying themselves at the same time."

"Well, I'm glad you enjoyed yourselves as much as the rest of us," Gisella said.

"Are we invited to see tomorrow's performance as well?" Tara said, remembering how the woman had mentioned they alternated the nightly performances between men and women.

"Absolutely," Gisella smiled. "You can stay as long as you want in our little village, as long as you're willing to join in the festivities along with the rest of our group."

"Oh, I'm willing to join in, alright," Jessop nodded as a long string of cum dangled out of his flagging organ down onto the stone floor of the stadium. "I'm already thinking about how I can up my game to have another shot at that pretty girl."

5

———

After the show, the three friends returned to their cabin, charged up and excited about what they'd seen, unable to stop gushing about the sexy performance. It wasn't just the sight of the pretty girl fingering herself in view of the entire crowd–they were already dreaming about what lay in store for them in future presentations.

"Can you *believe* that?" Clover said. "That might have been the sexiest thing I've ever seen."

"Watching a girl fingering herself?" Tara said.

"It was the whole spectacle of the thing," Clover nodded. "Watching a young woman expressing her sexuality for the first time. Her incredible figure. The flickering lights illuminating her body while she touched herself. And listening to the crowd show their appreciation while they watched her..."

"They were certainly demonstrating their appreciation in more ways than one," Jessop chuckled. "I've never seen so many people playing with themselves at the same time."

"It was pretty crazy," Tara nodded. "But can you blame

them? I could have come just rubbing myself against the stone step while I watched her getting off."

"What do you think the *next* performer is going to do?" Clover said. "I mean, there's only so many different ways a guy can stroke his dick. How are they going to keep it interesting every day?"

"I don't know," Jessop said. "But I'm already beginning to think of ways I can do it myself to have a shot at the couples' performance at the end of the month."

"Me too," Tara said. "Can you imagine how insane it would be to have sex with a thousand people watching you?"

"Not to mention having our turn with the sexiest member of the group," Clover nodded.

"We better turn in and put our thinking caps on," Tara said. "We've got the whole month to think of new ideas and show the old lady we're worthy contenders to participate in the games."

"It's more than just *Gisella* we're going to have to impress," Jessop chuckled. "We're going to need to come up with something novel and interesting enough to impress the whole group who'll be casting their votes."

"Well, we've certainly had enough kinky experiences traveling all the way from Norseland to Sotharius these past few months," Clover said. "It shouldn't be too hard to think of some techniques they've never seen before."

"Maybe they'll come to us in our dreams," Jessop said, lying down on their big solo bed and playing with his still-tingling tool absentmindedly.

"Well, don't keep us up all night playing with yourself," Clover said, lying down next to him and flopping over onto her stomach. "I want to be well rested for the next performance."

"Me too," Tara said, lying beside Clover and feeling her eyes already fluttering shut, spent from the day's excitement.

They pulled the bedcovers over their bodies, then they lay still in the darkness for a few moments, listening to the sound of crickets lulling them to sleep. But not before each of them had had another quiet orgasm, trying not to wake their bedmates as the two girls lay on their stomachs fingering their pussies and Jessop curled away to the other side, emptying his seed onto the straw floor while they all moaned softly.

W hen they awoke the following day, they joined Gisella and the rest of the tribe in the big amphitheater, queueing up to enjoy a fresh-cooked breakfast of poached eggs, sliced avocado, ripe cherry tomatoes, and fried bacon. As they dove into their delicious meal, they glanced around the stadium at the rest of the naked tribespeople, wondering which of the young men would be stepping up to the platform to display himself later that evening.

"Is it just me, or all of these people insanely *hot*?" Clover said, choking on one of her eggs.

"I've been noticing it too," Tara said. "With their caramel-colored skin and buff, toned bodies, it's like they're some kind of *super-race*."

"Not a single one of them has sagging tits or asses," Jessop nodded. "Even the *old* people have firm figures."

"Maybe it's from working the fields," Clover suggested, peering around the stadium at the lush gardens surrounding the courtyard.

"Or from constantly having *sex*," Tara laughed. "It doesn't look like they have many inhibitions, and lord knows

,they've got plenty enough opportunity with everyone running around naked."

"I'm not sure of the cause," Jessop said. "But I'm sure as hell interested in finding their magic elixir."

Suddenly, the old lady who sat with them previously approached from the front of the stadium, smiling at the three friends while she brought them three steaming cups of coffee.

"Did you sleep well last night after yesterday's performance?" she said.

"Like babies," Clover nodded.

"Very *noisy* babies," Tara smiled.

"I have to admit," Jessop grunted, his dick starting to twitch at the idea of watching a young man perform this time. "It was pretty hard to sleep, imagining what was coming next."

"Are you looking forward to watching a *boy* this time around?" Gisella said.

"Very much so," Clover said, darting her eyes over the buff figures of the young men assembled at the opposite corner of the amphitheater, with their thick appendages dangling between their thighs as they chatted among themselves.

"Have you thought about participating *yourselves*?" the old lady said. "If each of you are eighteen, technically you qualify to be part of the group. I'm sure the rest of our community would love to see what you bring to the table."

"It's crossed our minds," Jessop smiled. "The idea of hundreds of naked women watching me while I jerk off is quite a turn-on–"

"So it would appear," Gisella chuckled, watching his stiffening tool tilt toward one side of his thighs.

"What would you like us to do in the meantime?" Tara said. "That is, until this evening's performance?"

"You can help in the fields if you're interested," the old lady said. "There's plenty of soil to till and ripe fruit to pluck."

"We'll be happy to do all the tilling and plucking you like," Jessop grinned, peering at the swelling nipples and glistening vulvas of the young tribal women staring back at them.

After they finished breakfast, the friends joined the other tribespeople working in the fields, helping to gather fruit and vegetables with the supervision of the old woman watching them closely. It was hard to concentrate on the task at hand with so many beautiful young men and women constantly bending over, but they were each given an assigned task to gather a particular vegetable in their empty baskets.

Clover suddenly grunted, raising one of the sprouts for the others to see.

"I've never seen cucumbers this large before," she said, flaring her eyes. "This one must be at least ten inches long and three inches around."

"Mmm," Tara smiled, examining the phallic-shaped vegetable as she pulled a purple gourd from the ground. "I bet those are pleasant to enjoy in all *manner* of ways. Take a look at these aubergines. Talk about a perfect-sized dildo."

"What about these strange *pussy-shaped* plants?" Jessop said, shaking the top of a pink-colored flower shaped like a hollowed-out tube.

"Those are called pitcher plants," Gisella said, walking

up behind Jessop. "They're not to be harvested. They catch and kill insects and other animals that feed on the vegetables, like ants and rats."

"How does it *work* exactly?" Jessop said, running his finger around the inner lip of the plant, watching it flex and pucker gently.

"It uses a sticky syrup on the inside of the flower to attract its prey, then it closes up and tightens around the object, using its juices to slowly digest it."

"Gross," Jessop said, quickly pulling his finger out of the puckering plant before it tightened around his digit.

"Why do these plants grow so *large?"* Clover said, pulling a plush peach off one of the overhanging branches. "I've never such enormous fruit and vegetables in my travels."

"Maybe it's our fertile soil or because of the long growing season this close to the equator," the old lady said. "We've been blessed with a bounty that keeps us hearty and healthy all year round."

"I'll say," Jessop said, peering at the tight asses of the young tribeswomen as they worked the field and bent over to collect other provisions.

"Be sure to bring your baskets to the central square when you're finished," Gisella chuckled. "We're having curried lamb with eggplant stew for an early supper. You'll want to build up your strength for our next performance later tonight."

"I'm feeling invigorated already," Jessop grinned, his prick rising over the sexy flowers while he gawked at the beautiful naked tribeswomen.

6

———————

L ater that afternoon, the entire community gathered for another feast in the large amphithe- ater, then the three friends retired to their bedchamber to rest up for the evening's performance. When they returned to the stadium, Gisella had reserved their front-row seats once again as the rest of the crowd threaded into the bandstand, taking their seat on the tiered steps. The dais in the center of the ring had already been cleared and prepared with a fresh pile of soft animal rugs and flickering candles arranged around the perimeter of the stage. After the entire community had been seated and the sun had settled over the horizon, a hush fell over the theater while a tall shadow approached the rear of the stage.

"Uh!" Clover gasped when she saw one of the young tribesmen she'd been eyeing in the fields step closer toward the flickering light.

He was taller than most of the other men, with broad shoulders, carved pecs, and a ripped abdomen that framed the long appendage that swung between his thighs as he walked up the steps with his arms behind his back.

"Yes, please," Tara murmured to no one in particular while she ran her eyes over his buff figure and his chiseled face.

"That's a pretty impressive tool," Jessop nodded, unable to keep his own cock from twitching while he soaked up the perfect specimen. "It looks like it's not only the *vegetables* that grow big and firm around here."

"But why does he have his hands behind his back?" Clover said to the old woman, who'd chosen to sit beside Jessop for this evening's performance.

"He could be bringing a prop to assist in his performance," Gisella said. "We encourage our performers to use whatever objects aid in their arousal and fulfillment."

The young man walked toward the middle of the dais, then he paused while the crowd applauded softly, acknowledging his courage in stepping forward to share his intimate act for the rest of the group to enjoy. Then he brought his arms around the front of his body, revealing a cucumber unlike anything the trio had seen before. Perfectly straight and erect, with a girth of at least four inches in diameter and pushing one foot in length, it glistened in the flickering candlelight while the youth caressed it slowly, running his fingers up and down the shaft like he was stroking his cock.

"I never thought those things could be used for a *guy's* satisfaction before," Clover said, wrinkling her forehead in dismay. "I was too busy thinking about them as a dildo for my own use all this time."

"Maybe he's got similar intentions," Tara chuckled. "He's got a few orifices of his *own* he can stick that thing into if he feels so inclined."

"I'm not sure he could fit that thing in his mouth, let alone his *ass*," Jessop said, furrowing his brow while he pondered the possibilities.

"Maybe he's got something *else* in mind for it," Clover nodded, watching the young man starting to slide the cucumber down the front of his belly and over his swelling organ before slipping it between his thighs and rubbing it over his ass cheeks.

"Holy shit," Tara gushed, staring at his expanding dick. "His cock is almost as big as the *gherkin*."

"And it's not even fully hard yet," Clover smiled.

"Maybe he's a closet homosexual, and he prefers rubbing his cock against other guys' dicks," Jessop grunted, feeling his own organ growing in kind as he imagined frotting the jock's big erection with his own.

"I dunno," Tara said, shaking her head. "There's something about the way he's using it to stimulate the rest of his body that leads me to believe he has something else in mind for it."

As the handsome tribesman continued to slide the big tuber over his flexing muscles, his penis continued to harden until it was standing proudly straight and erect in a forty-five-degree upward angle.

"God, that's a beautiful cock," Clover panted, flapping her thighs in and out while sat transfixed watching the young man caress his body with the brightly colored vegetable. "I have no idea what he's planning to do with that thing, but if he ever needs any help caressing that big thumper of his, I'd be more than happy to help."

"Wait a little longer," Gisella said as she watched Jessop playing with his stiffening organ while he stared at the young man caressing his own body. "Something tells me he'll reveal his intentions soon enough..."

Suddenly, the youth grabbed both ends of the cucumber and twisted off the tip, placing the smaller piece on the floor of the platform. Then he squatted down and crossed his legs, turning the gourd around to show that it had been hollowed out to provide an open chamber roughly the size of his now fully erect organ."

"Holy shit," Tara said, widening her eyes. "He's going to fuck that thing like a *pussy*!"

"Do you think it will be big enough?" Clover said. "I mean, he's gotta be almost a foot long himself."

"I think we're about to find out," Tara said, sliding her hand over the front of her mound as she watched the hunk place the open end of the tuber over the tip of his glistening glans and slowly slide it down the length of his shaft.

"It's sad to see his beautiful cock disappearing from view, but you have to admit that's hot as *fuck*," Clover said, slipping two fingers into her dripping tunnel. "When I come back in my next life, I want to be that cucumber."

"No shit," Tara laughed, pressing her own fingers harder against her clit as she watched the youth moaning gently while he pumped the big tube over his embedded dick with two hands.

Jessop noticed something strange in the way the youth was holding the cucumber, and he turned toward Gisella with a curious expression.

"Why does he keep tapping the top of the tube with his thumb?" he said to the old woman, who was busy rubbing the side of her thigh against his as he rocked his hips up and down.

Gisella leaned forward a few inches and squinted at the dripping tuber, then she nodded her head softly.

"It looks like he's cut a small hole in the closed end of the cucumber to allow the release of trapped air. By holding his finger over the hole from time to time, he can control the amount of pressure building up inside the tube, providing extra suction to the glans of his penis."

"How ingenious," Jessop nodded, gripping his throbbing organ with two hands to mimic the action of the youth on the stage. "I'll have to try that sometime."

"We encourage our performers not to copy the techniques of the others as much as possible," the old lady said, wagging her finger. "It helps to keep our performances interesting while expanding our knowledge of new ways to pleasure ourselves."

"I was beginning to *wonder* how you'd be able to change it up day after day for an entire year," Clover nodded. "But after seeing the plethora of erotic plants growing in your garden, I'm beginning to think the possibilities are endless."

"Look," Tara suddenly grunted while she circled her nub in matching frequency with the youth's accelerating tube pumping. "It looks like he's getting close."

"How can you tell?" Clover huffed, jerking her fingers in and out of her pussy.

"His balls are starting to rise," Tara nodded, staring at the base of his dick disappearing in and out of the dripping tuber. "And a flush is beginning to spread over his chest."

"Good," Clover hissed, tickling the outsides of her labia with her index and little fingers as she fucked her pussy harder with her two middle fingers. "Because I'm just about ready to come along with him."

"Me too," Tara hissed, squeezing her right breast hard while she jilled herself furiously with her other hand.

Suddenly, the young man on the stage picked up the hollowed out tip of the cucumber that he'd placed beside him on the stage earlier, and he cupped it over his tightening balls, twisting it softly while he pumped the glistening tuber harder. As his sex flush spread rapidly over his neck and across his face, he arched his hips off the mat and tensed his whole body for a long moment, then he groaned deeply as a geyser of liquid shot out the tip of the cucumber, squirting his juices all over his heaving chest and quivering belly.

"Fuck me," Jessop grunted, shooting his load all over the top of Gisella's quivering thighs.

"I get first dibs," Tara gushed, squeezing her left hand so hard over her breast it looked like the nipple would explode.

"I'm the one who was gathering the *cucumbers* today," Clover laughed and grunted simultaneously. "If anyone should have the first shot at giving him a chance with some real sex, it should be me."

"You're going to have to be more creative than *that* to have a chance at coupling up with him at the end of the month," the old lady said. "There's still twenty-six performers ahead of you before we reveal the winners for the couple's exhibition. You better get busy dreaming up new ways to satisfy yourselves before the jury passes judgement."

"Oh, I'll be getting busy, alright," Clover panted, gradually beginning to recover from another intense orgasm. "I spent the whole *night* dreaming up some kinky ways to impress your judges."

7

After the trio enjoyed the boy-with-cucumber performance, they went back to their cabin to brainstorm ideas for their own public demonstrations. They knew they'd have to come up with something new and exotic if they were going to stay one step ahead of the young tribespeople who had the advantage of witnessing something different every day. But they'd just come from the land of Sannyans, where the animated stone sculptures at the erotic temple had taught them hundreds of interesting new positions and techniques for both single and paired stimulation. The nude tribespeople weren't the only ones who had a few tricks up their sleeve.

"That was pretty hot watching that guy using a *legume* to get off," Clover said as they hopped onto the bed, facing one another in a cross-legged position.

"Yeah," Tara nodded. "It looks like we can use props to augment our performance. That opens up a whole new world of possibilities."

"What about using that sexy *flower* we found in the field today?" Jessop said. "It might only work for a *guy*, but I'd be more than happy to experiment with it when no one's looking."

"Something tells me they've already tried that before," Tara chuckled. "Besides, the old lady said that plant is hands-off for harvesting. How would you carry a live one onto the stage?"

"Okay," Jessop frowned. "How about if I built one of those crazy *fucking machines* we saw at the seven dwarfs' house? It's hard to imagine anyone else designing such a unique device for their own self-stimulation."

"That thing was driven by a water-wheel connected to an adjacent stream," Clover said, shaking her head. "It would be hard enough for you to build one with the materials they have on hand in this settlement, beyond the difficulty of keeping it a secret until the day of the performance. I think it's best we stick to the tried-and-true methods of stimulating ourselves."

"It doesn't sound like the old lady's been very impressed with what we've demonstrated so far while we watched the others perform in the theater," Tara said. "It's going to have to be something completely different from anything they've seen before."

The trio paused for a moment while they darted their eyes over each other's bodies as they reflected back on their various exotic journeys through the land of Abbynthia.

"What about the *self-sucking* pose we learned from the Sannyans at their erotic temple?" Jessop said. "That requires a special technique with plenty of practice to pull it off properly. Not everybody would be able to do that."

"That would be pretty fucking hot for the whole group to watch," Clover nodded while she rubbed her heel absent-mindedly against her moistening pussy.

"Yes, but only if it hasn't already been done by one of the

members of the group," Tara said. "Or it won't be displayed again before we have our chance. With the size of some of these dudes' dicks, I wouldn't be surprised if they didn't beat us to the punch."

"Not if it was a *woman* performing the act," Jessop smiled, staring down at the girls' glistening pussies. "That's a one-in-a-million acrobatic technique that very few people could pull off."

"True," Tara replied. "But if you remember, we had a little help licking our pussies from the Sannyans assisting with some extra pressure. In this case, we're going to have to perform it entirely alone on the stage."

"Maybe you just need to *practice* a little more to stretch your body that few extra inches," Jessop said.

Tara paused for a moment as she turned toward Clover, who was nodding excitedly at the idea.

"Well, there's technically *two* of us who could pull it off, and only one who can introduce it to the people," she said. "Which one of us should be the guinea pig?"

"You're shorter and more flexible than me," Clover nodded. "You can bend your spine more easily to reach your own pussy. I think it should be *you* for this one."

"Okay," Tara said. "Now we just need to think of something equally novel and exciting for you guys to show the crowd–"

"We can worry about that another day," Clover smiled. "Why don't we get started working on your flexibility? You're a bit rusty after sitting idle these past few days watching the others getting off. Now it's *your* turn."

"Right, then," Jessop nodded as his cock began to twitch and harden at the thought of watching Tara suck her own pussy again. "Why don't you position yourself behind Tara's back while I help to pull her legs over her shoulders? That way, she'll have two extra targets to shoot for—my cock resting only inches away from her head, and your mouth positioned directly over her slit."

"Works for me," Clover said, turning toward Tara. "Are you ready to give it another try, Tara?"

"You're reading my mind," Tara grinned, throwing her legs over her shoulders and rolling onto her back as she peered up at her friends with a sliver of lubrication dripping out of her pussy and over the front of her belly.

The next day, the three friends continued assisting in the fields by collecting more fruit and vegetables for their cold storage locker, then they retired to their quarters to prepare for the evening's next erotic performance. When they arrived at the stadium, Gisella was already waiting at their usual spots and they sat next to her, with Jessop wedged in between the two girls.

"It's a pleasure to see you again," the old woman smiled. "Are you well rested for tonight's performance?"

"As well rested as we can be after toiling in the sun all day," Clover said.

"I hope you've had a chance for a little R&R to rest your bodies and get in the mood for our show. It would be a shame not to enjoy the performance to its fullest potential."

"Don't worry," Tara grinned. "We've had *plenty* of R&R to help get us in the mood."

"Have you been trying out any of the new techniques you've seen on our stage?" Gisella smiled.

"Those and a few other new techniques," Clover nodded.

"Good," the old lady said. "I think you're going to enjoy

this evening's performance. It features one of our most agile participants."

"That sounds interesting," Tara said, wrinkling her forehead while she worried this new performer could be stealing some of her thunder.

As the sun began to lower behind the mountains in the distance, one of the tribesmen pounded a large drum, gradually increasing the pace while a young woman strolled toward the back of the illuminated platform. When she ascended the steps and stopped in the middle of the dais, the drummer pounded the drum loudly one last time to signal the performance was about to begin. The girl paused, facing the crowd with her hands clenched in a fist in front of each of her thighs.

"She doesn't look very relaxed preparing to touch herself in front of the crowd," Clover said to Gisella.

"Give her time," the old lady replied. "Every performer opens up in their own way with their own special surprises."

The three friends scanned her petite figure, running their eyes up and down the entire length of her body, from her long, soft hair to her pretty toenails, painted a brilliant shade of crimson red. Her breasts were small and round with long pointy nipples, their shadows dancing over her orbs from the flickering candles surrounding her naked body. She had a crease running down the front of her toned abdomen, which seemed all the more highlighted from the shadows of the candles and her immaculately shaved mound. Her legs were slender but shapely, displaying a thin gap between the top of her parted thighs to reveal a small pink appendage jutting out from the top of her glistening labia.

"My God," Tara gushed, squeezing her legs together next

to Jessop, whose dick was steadily rising as he soaked up the girl's athletic and ripped body. "She's a specimen."

"Yeah," Jessop nodded. "I could work with that."

"You mentioned she's especially *agile*," Clover said to Gisella sitting next to her. "What do you think she's going to do?"

"It will become apparent soon enough," the old lady smiled. "The night is just getting started."

While the girl remained rigid as a statue, the crowd applauded her softly, encouraging her to begin her performance. Suddenly, she raised her hands over her hips, then she turned them with her palms facing up and slowly uncurled her fingers, revealing two round, polished stones roughly one inch in diameter.

"Okay," Tara nodded, squinting her eyes in curiosity. "I'm not exactly sure what she's going to do with those..."

The girl rolled the stones onto the tips of her fingers, then she raised them to her breasts, sliding them sensuously around the edges of her flared nipples while she stared out into the crowd. Tara could have sworn she was peering directly at her, and it was a bit unnerving watching her expressionless face as she continued stimulating her nipples. After a minute or so, the girl paused the movement of the stones, then she placed each one on top of her swelling teats, balancing them carefully as she lowered her hands back down to the sides of her hips.

"Impressive," Tara nodded while the crowd applauded appreciatively and the girl curled her lips slowly upward while staring at the sexy elf.

Tara wasn't sure if it was the pointed ears poking out of her pink-hued hair, or the fact that she was sitting almost directly in front of the sexy girl that made her focus entirely on her, but either way, she was becoming increasingly turned on by her attention, slowly spreading her legs to reveal her glistening vulva and the drops of fluid running down the crack of her ass.

"Those tits look seriously *fuckable*," Clover said, leaning over Jessop's upturned pole to whisper in Tara's ear.

"Yeah," Jessop nodded, overhearing Clover's comment. "But something tells me this pretty native girl only has eyes for Tara."

Tara nodded and raised her fingers to twist her own bullets, making them harden and swell, then the native girl lifted her hands to grasp each of the stones again, slowly sliding them down the crease of her stomach and over the crest of her hips toward the diamond-shaped opening between her legs illuminated by the candles at the back of the stage.

"Fuck the cucumber," Tara panted as she moved her own hands down the front of her body to mimic the action of the girl on the stage. "When I come back, I want to come back as those *stones*."

"She's just getting started," Gisella chuckled. "You have no idea–"

Suddenly the girl flexed her legs and lowered herself onto the soft sheepskin rugs covering the front of the stage, gradually parting her legs as she bent her knees. The crowd could clearly see her glistening pussy now with its shaved lips, swelling softly in the light of the flickering candles. She curled the stones around the insides of each of her parted thighs, then she dragged them one at a time from the base of her dripping slit along the opening to the tip of her swelling clit, which by this point was poking almost a full inch out of its hood, gleaming proudly in the light of the surrounding candles.

"Oh my God," Clover shuddered as she played with her own hardening nub. "I could suck that bean all day."

"Hands off, girl," Tara hissed back at her. "She's all mine."

While the pretty girl continued staring at Tara, she wedged her flaring gland between the two stones and rolled them softly between her cupped hands as she tilted her head back and licked her parted lips sensuously.

"Fuck me," Tara groaned, twisting her own bulb between her fingers to demonstrate her appreciation for the girl's sexy performance. "Who knew rubbing two stones against your body could be this much fun?"

"Just *wait,*" the old lady said, smiling at Tara. "The best is still to come."

"I thought each of these performances was supposed to be new, and the crowd had no advance knowledge of what was to come?" Tara said.

"We don't," Gisella smiled. "That doesn't mean we haven't experimented with similar techniques on our *own* time."

Tara turned her attention back to the girl on the stage, and her eyes widened when she saw her sliding the stones back down the front of her slit and slipping them one after the other into her dripping vulva.

"What is she doing *now*?" Jessop said to the old lady while he gripped his throbbing cock in a vice-grip as he watched the nubile girl roll backwards and raise each of her bent legs over her shoulders, then interlocking her feet behind her head.

"Watch and learn," Gisella said. "She's going to rock her hips to make the balls bounce together inside her cavity as they stimulate her X-spot."

"You mean her *G-spot*?" Clover said, peering at her with pinched eyebrows.

"Is that what you call it?" the old lady said. "It's the most sensitive place on the inside of her chamber, corresponding to the location of her squirt gland."

"Holy shit," Jessop said, moving his hips in kind with the girl on the stage as she began to rock back and forth with louder groans. "That's insane. I didn't know a girl could get off without touching herself directly..."

"You're about to see just how well this works," Gisella said, stroking the top of Clover's shaking thigh while she trilled her clit next to the old woman.

"Look," Clover panted as she began to see a steady stream of fluid beginning to leak out of the girl's orifice and down the crack of her ass while her labia slowly parted. "I think she's getting ready to come."

"Watch her pucker closely," the old lady nodded. "When you see it beginning to expand then starting to spasm in successive pulses, you'll know she's reached the point of climax."

"What about the *balls*?" Tara said, staring at the girl's dripping perineum as she circled her clit furiously. "Is she going to keep them inside?"

"You're about to find out soon enough," Gisella smiled.

Suddenly, the pretty native girl took a deep intake of air and clenched her face tightly as it reddened a deep shade of crimson, and she flexed her legs tighter around her torso, pausing in mid-swing. As the three friends gawked at her upturned pussy in delirious rapture on the edge of their own powerful climaxes, the girl suddenly jetted the two stone balls violently out of her flexing pussy directly in the direction of Tara. Before she even had a chance to react, they bounced off each of her shaking tits and ricocheted upward before they bounced noisily back onto the stone floor of the auditorium and rolled to a stop in front of the shaking native girl. Tara peered back at her with eyes as wide as saucers, and the girl grinned softly, winking with one eye.

"I think she's trying to tell you something," Clover laughed, pulling her fingers out of her spasming pussy.

"Yeah," Jessop grunted, holding his spent dick in his hands while she stared at the native girl still tied up in a knot on the stage. "Like she wants to play *catch* with you or something."

"I'll be happy to oblige," Tara panted, rubbing the small indentations on her tits where the girl had expertly aimed her projectiles.

"I guess it's back to the drawing board," Clover said, peering at her two friends. "This girl has seriously raised the bar in terms of what we'll have to bring to the table to keep up with their performances."

"I've already got *mine* figured out," Tara nodded. "But I'm starting to get some new ideas for each of you. It's going to be an interesting twenty-four hours before the start of the next performance."

"I hope we're given you some interesting ideas to expand your horizons," the old lady smiled. "Does this mean you'll be staying with us a little longer?"

"Definitely until the end of the month anyway," Clover nodded. "We're hoping to participate in the grand finale before the turn of the new moon."

"You better start getting ready then," Gisella said, peering up at the crescent moon rising higher in the evening sky. "There's only a few weeks left before we reveal the winners."

8

After the improvised ben-wa-balls performance, the three friends returned to their cabin to discuss some more ideas for their own upcoming demonstrations. They were beginning to become worried by the increasingly divergent presentations of the young tribal members that there would be nothing left for them to show when it came time for their turn.

"Okay," Tara said, stretching out on the mattress beside Clover and Jessop. "We've got to think of something different for Clover to do now. There's only so many different things we can stuff into our pussy before the audience gets tired of us using props."

Clover paused for a moment while she pondered the possibilities and reflected back on her kinky encounters with the different native peoples she'd met along the trio's long journey.

"What if we don't use any props at all?" she said, darting her eyes upward with a guilty expression.

"What do you mean?" Tara said. "What could you possibly do that these people haven't already tried?"

"Well, I've been checking out the bodies of all these naked tribespeople," Clover said. "And everybody is plainly all-male or all-female–"

"Of course," Jessop said, wrinkling his brow in confusion. "What else would they be?"

"They've probably never seen a *transgender* person before."

"True, but you've already had a couple of turns at that, and we don't exactly have another mage or magic deity standing by this time to transform you back into one," Tara said.

"Yes," Clover said. "But I do have a few magic globes of my *own* to work with–"

She reached into a pouch resting on the floor beside their clothes in the corner of the room and pulled out two glistening orbs emitting a mysterious glow about them.

"Remember when that mage in the tavern in Longdale used his magic powers to satisfy my wish to become a shemale for a couple of days?"

"Yes, but that was a long time ago, and he must be a million miles away by now..."

"True, but he slipped a little consolation prize into my pocket before we left the Cock and Hen bar. He said whenever I rub these little balls together a certain way, I can reanimate as a ladyboy for twenty-four hours whenever I want."

"He *what*?" Tara said, glaring at Clover with angled eyebrows. "And you've been holding this back from us all this time?"

"Well, he said I had to be careful about using them too often. If I overused them two frequently, it could transform me into a goat or a snake. So obviously, I've been keeping them in standby for a special occasion."

"Holy *shit*, Clover," Jessop gushed. "That's insane! You look so hot with a big dick in place of your pussy."

"Thanks a lot," Clover frowned, peering at Jessop with a wrinkled forehead.

"It's not that I *prefer* you as a boy," Jessop backpedaled, throwing up his hands in defense. "It's just that with all of your other features staying the same, you look pretty fucking sexy with big tits, a pretty face, and an hourglass figure coming along with the package. A lot of guys and girls fantasize about getting it on with a tranny."

"I bet these sheltered tribespeople would freak out if walked up onto that stage with a big swinging dick dangling between your legs," Tara nodded.

"Maybe so," Clover said. "But what if it doesn't work when I get up there? Or these crystals turn me into a *goat* for the rest of my life?"

"I guess there's only one way to be sure," Jessop grinned. "You'll have to practice in the safety of your own private cabin before you go public with your new powers."

"How exactly did the mage tell you to use them before we left the tavern?" Clover said, squinting warily at the glowing orbs.

"He said to hold them together in one hand while I rolled one ball around the other for a few minutes..."

"Did he say which *color* to circle around the other?" Jessop said, noticing one ball was pink-colored and the other was colored a shade of teal-blue.

"I don't think it matters," Clover said. "At least he didn't mention that to me."

"It doesn't sound that complicated to me," Tara nodded. "Maybe you should just try it gently for a few moments and see if you recognize any familiar feelings. You can always stop if you feel anything strange going on–"

"You mean like growing a *cock* between my legs?" Clover chuckled.

"Or little horns coming out of your head..."

"Very funny," Clover huffed, punching Tara playfully in her shoulder.

"It's up to you," Jessop said. "We can always look for *other* novel ways to impress the judges."

"No," Clover said. "I've been meaning to give this a try for some time now. It's now or never."

"Okay," Tara said, clasping Clover's hands gently. "Is there anything we can do to help?"

"Just get ready to slap the balls out of my hands if you notice me growing scales on my skin," Clover chuckled.

"No worries," Jessop said. "We don't want to be traipsing around the countryside with a goat in tow for the rest of our travels. Even if you could provide us with a never-ending supply of milk–"

"I'm going to *kill* you guys if you keep this up," Clover said, staring at Jessop with daggers in her eyes.

"Okay," Jessop nodded, putting a serious expression back on his face. "Just concentrate on what you want while you roll the balls around in your hand."

Clover took a deep breath, then she closed her eyes while she rolled the fingers of her right hand slowly, turning the balls around one another while she cupped her palm. One of the orbs almost fell out when it slid too close to the edge, and Clover grabbed her hand, forcing her to stop for a moment.

"Maybe you should do this with your eyes open," she said, shaking her head.

"Yeah," Jessop nodded. "And use *both* hands to turn the balls around each other."

"Fine," Clover huffed, staring down at the two balls

beginning to glow brighter and beginning to burn warmer in her palm.

She cupped her right hand tighter, then she took the index finger of her other hand and slowly moved the pink ball around the perimeter of the teal-blue one, watching the smoky ether emanating from her palm rise higher in the air.

"Are you feeling anything yet?" Clover said, darting her eyes between Clover's vacant face and her rumbling stomach.

"I'm beginning to feel a tingling in my crotch," Clover nodded. "And some pressure building up between my thighs–"

"I guess that's a *good* sign, right?" Jessop said, placing his hands over Clover's knees and gently pressing them further apart.

"Mmm," Clover nodded, beginning to breathe harder. "It's starting to feel good down there, like somebody's stimu-lating my clit."

Tara and Jessop sat transfixed while they stared at Clover's tingling pussy, widening their eyes as they watched the tiny gland at the top of her folds gradually growing in size and pushing out from its hood while her labia began to swell and close up, forming a bulbous sack between her legs. When the glass orbs finally stopped glowing and shaking in her hand, she peered down between her legs, staring at an eight-inch hard-on bobbing up over her tight nutsack.

"Holy *fuck*," she said, grabbing hold of her new dick and squeezing it gently to make sure it was real. "I swear, it's even bigger than last time!"

"Does it feel good when you touch it?" Tara said.

"Yeah," Clover panted. "Like five times better than when I touch my clit."

"That's probably because it's more than five times as *big* as your regular clit," Tara chuckled.

"What about here?" Jessop said, reaching down to cup her testicles and rubbing them softly.

"Huh!" Clover nodded, swiping his hand away from her ladyboy parts. "Yeah, that only makes it feel worse. I'm mean even *better*. This thing seems to have a mind of its own."

"Tell me about it," Jessop grunted, suddenly realizing his own dick had grown hard as a rock watching Tara transform into a sexy ladyboy. "You've got the best of both worlds. You still look like a sexy woman, but you've got an impressive dick to use anyway you like."

"Did you want to test it out to make sure everything works the way it's supposed to?" Tara said, smiling at Clover with a flushed face while her pussy began to form a wet spot between her legs on the edge of the bed.

"You mean by *fucking* one of you guys, straight up?" she said, twitching her cock while she stared at Tara's parted labia and dripping slit.

"Or *both* of us at the same time..." Jessop said, raising his eyebrows.

"You mean your favorite way when there's two cocks involved?" Clover smiled back at him.

"Maybe," he grinned like a Cheshire Cat. "If you feel up to it."

"Well, it seems that my *dick* sure as hell does," Clover chuckled, peering down at her bobbing organ starting to emit a drop of pre-cum out of its slit while her balls grew even tighter around the base of her shaft.

"What do you say, Tara?" Jessop said, glancing toward his other friend. "Are you ready to give both of us a little pussy massage at the same time?"

"I think I might remember how to do that," Tara nodded,

reflecting back on how she'd fucked the sexy duo at the Sannyan temple when she sat over their connected dicks.

Jessop wasted no time shifting his body in front of Clover and pushing his hips forward until his upturned pole pressed against Clover's, then he wrapped his legs around the back of her ass and leaned backward onto his outstretched arms.

"I think there's enough room for you to squeeze in here," he smiled toward Tara, who was already up on her knees, preparing to sit on their cocks.

"Hold them together while I squat over of you," she grunted, turning to face Clover as she swung one knee in the gap between their torsos and positioned her flaring pussy over the tips of their joined tools.

When she began to lower herself slowly over their thick shafts, the three of them groaned loudly, remembering the exquisite feeling of fucking themselves in one joined position while they caressed and kissed each other's tingling bodies.

"Oh fuck," Clover gasped when Tara lifted her hands to squeeze Clover's shaking breasts and began to rock her hips up and down over their throbbing tools. "I can't help it, I'm going to come already. Uh, uh, *unghhh...*"

As Clover's body began to shake and convulse against her friends' bodies, Tara kissed her on her lips while Jessop spread his arms around their backs, holding all of them together tightly.

"That didn't take long," Tara chuckled when Clover's breathing began to return to normal and she peered up at her friends sheepishly.

"Sorry about that," Clover said. "I'm just not used to having a big cock between my legs again, and it's been a while since I've felt a warm pussy caressing my organ."

"No worries," Tara laughed. "But you're going to need a little more practice so you don't pop off so quickly in front of the entire community in the big grandstand. I don't think you'll win any prizes lasting only a few seconds while they get all worked up watching you work your oversize prick."

"I suppose not," Clover sighed, still feeling her hard-on pulsing as it nestled next to Jessop's throbbing tool in Tara's tunnel. "Just give me a second to recover my energy before we give it another go. I'm pretty sure I can long enough to let each of you get off before I pop the cork again."

"Okay," Tara said, squeezing Clover's and Jessop's mashed dicks together as she flexed her perineal muscles. "Just give me the word when you're ready, and you can gush your champagne all over the insides of my dripping pussy and Jessop's throbbing dick."

"I'm *ready*," Clover nodded, lowering her face toward's Tara's tits and taking each of her swollen nipples into her mouth while biting on them gently. "I could come all night this way if you guys are up for it."

"I'm glad *one* of us can," Jessop groaned as Tara began humping their joined cocks once again. "I've already emptied my balls once today. I don't have your stamina, with an adolescent's raging hormones and your newfound man equipment. Let's try to make this one last a little longer..."

9

Shortly before dusk, the trio returned to the amphitheater to join Gisella in her front-row seat to prepare for the next erotic performance. Clover decided to wear a short sarong over her hips this time to cover up her new ladyboy tool, which the mage from Longdale had said could last as long as twenty-four hours. The old lady smiled when she saw three friends approaching, with Clover choosing to sit at the far end of the group to conceal her little secret.

"It's nice to see you again," Gisella said when they sat down next to her. "Are you ready for a little *boy* action tonight?"

"If he's anything like your *last* male performer," Tara nodded. "I expect he won't be so little."

"We're definitely ready for some more *cock strutting*," Clover said. "I think Jessop needs a little more inspiration before he's ready to go public with his own public display."

"Really?" Gisella said, staring down at his cum-coated cock from their latest three-way hookup in the cabin. "It looks to me like he's been getting plenty worked up reliving the three performances he's seen so far. Which ones have excited you the most?"

"All of them," Jessop grinned. "I'm enjoying the thought of hooking up with any one of them if I have a chance at the end of the month."

"We'll have to see about that," the old lady smiled as she rubbed her thigh softly against his. "It would have to be some exceptional performances from the men to arrange a same-sex hookup for the winners."

"Well, we've got a few surprises planned that might open your judges' eyes," Jessop nodded, feeling his tool beginning to twitch again when he noticed a shadow moving toward the rear of the stage while the pre-performance drumbeat began to slowly escalate in volume and pace. Then his eyes flared when he saw a handsome youth walking onto the stage carrying a familiar plant.

"Is that what I *think* it is?" he said, peering at the tubular flower hanging upside down from its tall stem rising up from a large clay pot.

"If you mean a *pitcher plant*, yes," Gisella nodded.

"I thought you said we weren't allowed to harvest those plants?" Jessop said, furrowing his brow.

"I meant in the sense of not *killing* it," the old lady said. "In this case, the young man has carefully uprooted it and placed it in nurturing soil for subsequent replanting."

"If I'd known that," Jessop grunted. "I would have been practicing with it a lot more in the meantime."

"You'll still have plenty of chances while working in the fields if you enjoy his performance," Gisella grinned.

"I'm beginning to get in the mood already," Jessop nodded as his penis started to stiffen while he watched the youth place the pot at the front of the stage and position his dangling organ over the tip of the flower.

The blossom undulated for a few moments, apparently noticing the presence of some fresh prey in its proximity, then it slowly began to angle upward, spreading its lips wider to invite the organism to taste its sweet fruit. The young man slapped his pole against the sides of its soft petals, rubbing it gently against the silky texture until it was completely erect, bobbing excitedly in front of the puckering opening.

"It's strange how the plant seems to sense that something edible is in its presence," Tara nodded, squinting at the strangely shaped plant. "Are you sure it's not going to *hurt* him when he puts his member inside?"

"Not if it's only in there for a few minutes," Gisella chuckled. "It takes quite a few days for this kind of plant to fully digest its prey, especially one as large as that one."

"Yes," Clover said, sliding her hands over the front of her sarong to keep her swelling instrument from poking up between her legs. "It's pretty impressive for such a young man."

"Our boys are quite well endowed," Gisella nodded, darting her eyes between Jessop's impressive instrument and the youth's on the stage. "Whether it's from all the excitement of building up to this moment, or from their frequent practice preparing for this first public display, I couldn't be sure..."

"Something tells me he's tried this a couple times before," Tara chuckled, watching the young man angle his flaring tool into the opening of the plant as it clamped down over his glans.

The youth tilted his head back and moaned as the plant began flexing and pulling his organ deeper into its cavity with rhythmic contractions along the length of its tube-shaped shaft.

"If I didn't know any better," Clover said, crossing her legs trying to keep her rising erection at bay. "I'd think the shape of that plant adapted for this precise purpose. It seems to fit his swelling organ like a *glove*."

"The oblong shape is designed to capture and digest all manner of organisms, from insects and frogs to rats and snakes," Gisella nodded.

"Well, that's one impressively long *snake* the plant is swallowing right now," Clover panted, squeezing her thighs against her throbbing hard-on.

"What happens now that he's got it inserted all the way?" Jessop said as his own hard-on bounced up against his stomach while he imagined fucking the sensuous flower himself.

"The flower clamps down over the base and surrounds his shaft with a tingly fluid designed to aid in digestion," Gisella said.

"All the while pulsing and squeezing along the length of his erection?" Tara said, noticing the flower flexing while it squeezed the tribal boy harder.

"Yes," Gisella nodded. "The movement helps to break down the organism trapped inside while it's juices finishes the job."

"He doesn't seem to be mind being trapped inside this carnivorous plant at all," Clover grinned, feeling her erection trying to free its binds and rub against the silky fabric of her sarong.

"I understand it feels quite similar to the sensation of a woman's vagina stimulating a man's organ," the old lady said. "I suspect there's a reason why so many of them have been planted in the fields by our young tribespeople."

"I can't wait to get my hands on one again," Jessop nodded, twisting his fist slowly over the top of his dripping glans while he watched the young tribesman rocking his hips back and forth over the swinging plant as it flexed its stem harder to resist his movement. "Not to mention my aching *dick*–"

"Do you want to see what it feels like?" Gisella said, dipping the tips of her fingers into her moist pussy then cupping them together over his bobbing pole.

"Yes please," Jessop grunted, staring at her dripping hands while he arched his hips upward.

As he began rocking his hips in concert with the moaning youth on the stage, the three friends panted in unison while they rocked, tribbed, and thrust their hips forward, feeling their own pleasure rising in synchronicity with the sexy youth flexing his abs as he swung the plant back and forth on its rocking base.

"Jesus," Clover panted, unable to keep her swelling erection from poking up higher in her tenting sarong. "I could use some of that *myself* right now–"

"So I can see," the old lady said, turning her head to glance at her big tentpole while squeezing Jessop's organ harder between her hands as he pumped his dick faster in her palms. "It seems that you've been hiding a little something *extra* from me these past few performances..."

"You mean *this*?" she said, leaning forward in an unsuccessful attempt to cover up her big erection flapping against her belly. "This popped up earlier today when we were brainstorming ideas for some novel demonstrations of our own."

"Well, I think you should do *more* of that whenever you have the chance," Gisella smiled, interlacing her fingers while Jessop's glistening helmet poked in and out of her hands. "Because it looks like the three of you have got a few extra talents to share with the rest of us."

"Oh *fuck*," Jessop hissed, staring down at his dick while Gisella squeezed it between her hands. "I can't hold it any longer. This is too insane–"

"Watching a boy stick his dick in a plant?" Gisella said. "Or watching your friends touching themselves while they get off at the same time?"

"Both," Jessop said, arching his back as he felt his tightening load beginning to shoot up his shaft. "Ahhhh!"

Right around the time Jessop began shooting long strings of come all over his heaving chest and Gisella's clamping hands, the young man on the stage suddenly jerked his body forward, rocking his torso back and forth while he emptied his seed deep inside the suckling plant. It seemed to take him almost a full minute to recover from his extended orgasm, then when he finally stopped moving, the dripping flower relaxed its mouth and spit his spent tool out of its opening, slowly shriveling back to its usual size and drooping down over the front of the stage, dripping long strings of liquid onto the platform.

"Do they *always* let go of it after the man ejaculates?" Tara said, pulling her fingers out of her own spasming and dripping vulva.

"Yes," the old lady said, staring down at Jessop's pulsating crown as she loosened her grip on his organ. "I don't think they're fully accustomed to the pH balance of a man's semen, which seems to interfere with their digestion. It's almost as if they recognize the young man is using it for his *own* satisfaction, rather than the other way around."

"That's a good thing," Clover grunted, wiping her spent seed over the front of her sarong as she tilted her detumescing cock back between her legs. "Because I'd hate for that thing to swallow my new willy before I've had a chance to display for the amusement of the rest of the tribe."

"You'd best keep that thing under cover until you're ready to go public with it later this month," Gisella nodded. "The more of a surprise it is when you eventually reveal it, the better your chances of winning the admiration of the crowd for most original performance."

"Oh, I plan on keeping it under wraps alright," Clover nodded. "This thing has a limited shelf life and comes with a few unexpected side effects. I won't be placing it anywhere it doesn't belong until I'm fully ready."

10

The following day, the three friends returned to working the fields after another long, communal breakfast. A few hours later, Jessop disappeared into the woods for an extended absence, and Clover and Tara peered at one another with a quizzical expression.

"What's going on with Jess?" Clover said, pinching her eyebrows together. "I haven't seen him since the morning meal."

"Maybe he's looking for some more of those *erotic plants* to play with, away from everybody's prying eyes," Tara chuckled. "He seemed to enjoy the show even more than usual last night."

"That's because he was getting a little extra attention," Clover smiled. "Maybe he's searching for a few lonely tribespeople to test out his ideas."

"Is that even allowed?" Tara said. "I got the feeling from the old lady that the young people were supposed to be *hands off* until they were ready to go public."

"I'm not sure that applies to the ones who've already

popped their cherry, in a manner of speaking. If anything, their coming out is designed to encourage *more* creative mingling among the tribe. I'm sure he's happy to do his part spreading the word, if not his seed."

"I was kind of looking forward to spreading some of my *own* seeds today," Clover frowned, caressing the tops of the erotic pitcher plants sitting dormant in the field.

Tara glanced down at her bare lower body, no longer covered by the short sarong, noticing her ladyboy cock had disappeared, replaced by her usual glistening slit.

"It seems that you'll have to wait for your next reanimation," she smiled.

"I think I should save that for a chance at the big prize," Clover nodded, peering at the buff bodies of the naked tribespeople working alongside them in the field. "I don't want to push my luck using my quota of transformations before I have a chance to try it on some of these sexy natives."

"Are you looking to hookup with a boy or a girl?" Tara said, staring at Clover's swollen nipples while she glanced furtively around her.

"It hardly matters," Clover smiled. "Every one of them is insanely beautiful and extremely creative in the ways they express their sexuality."

"I wonder what the next performer will show us tonight?" Tara nodded. "I'm already getting turned on just imagining what she might pull out of her hat this time–"

"Or put *in*," Clover chuckled. "They seem to be coming increasingly bold in finding new devices to play with."

"Why don't we go see if we can find Jessop?" Tara said. "At the very least, we can take a little break and have a little tête-à-tête when nobody's looking. I haven't experienced the lovely feeling of a slippery pussy rubbing up against mine since we left the erotic temple."

"You're reading my mind, girl," Clover nodded, watching the dribbles of shiny fluid running down the insides of Tara's thighs.

~

L ater that evening, the trio made their way back to the main auditorium in the middle of the square, preparing to watch another erotic performance by one of the young tribespeople. Tara glanced down at Jessop's bare torso, noticing some strange welts on the back of his ass and his lower mound.

"What were you doing, hiding away in the forest all morning?" she said. "It looks like you were traipsing through some pretty heavy brush."

"I was looking for some new exotic plants to add to my repertoire," Jessop grinned.

"Did you find anything as perfectly suited as the sucking pitcher plant?" Clover laughed. "I'm kind of disappointed that I missed my own chance to give it a try while I had the opportunity to dip my meat into its trap."

"Even *better*," Jessop nodded. "Something that provides an entirely *different* kind of stimulation, wherever I want it."

"Do tell," Clover said, peering at him with a wrinkled forehead. "Don't keep it from the *rest* of us while we're watching everybody else getting off. Tara and I are dying to try out some of these new techniques for ourselves."

"All in due time," Jessop smiled. "I'm saving it for the big show, so everyone can share in the new technique once it's revealed."

"You're such a *tease*," Tara laughed as she waved to Gisella, who was waiting for them at their reserved seats in front of the grandstand.

"Good to see you again," the old lady smiled when she saw them approaching. "Did you have a restful evening and a productive day?"

"If by productive, you mean interesting and stimulating," Clover said. "I'd have to say yes. Your little village of Whisperwood is full of surprises."

"I'm glad you're finding a way to expand your horizons," Gisella nodded, pinching her eyes at Jessop's scuffed lower extremities. "What about *you*, Jessop? Have you been exploring some new territories of your own?"

"Indeed I have," he smiled at the old lady. "In fact, I've discovered a new way to stimulate myself that I think your fellow tribespeople might find quite interesting. Do you think you might be able to fit me into the schedule for an erotic performance of my own during the next opening?"

"You're in luck," Gisella nodded. "It just so happens that there's no one coming of age tomorrow, so if you're willing to go public tomorrow night, we might be able to squeeze you in."

Suddenly, they heard a rumbling sound coming from the front of the auditorium, and the three friends' attention returned to the stage as the drummer's thumping began to rise and two buff tribal members lifted a heavy object onto the middle of the dais. They peered at the strange object rocking softly on the platform, then Clover glanced at Gisella sitting next to her, wrinkling her brow.

"A *rocking horse*?" she said. "How can the next presenter possibly use that to aid her erotic performance?"

"You're about to find out," the old lady smiled. "Our

young people are very creative in finding new ways to stimulate themselves in the absence of an available partner."

"So we're beginning to *see*," Tara chuckled. "Though we were hoping to provide them with some suitable partners of our own, soon enough."

As the drummer began to increase the intensity of his drumming, another naked tribal girl ascended the back of the stage, then she walked over next to the wooden horse. The audience applauded politely, then she placed her hand on the carved, upright neck of the effigy and rocked it slowly forward and back. Suddenly a long, phallic-shaped device began bobbing up from a hole in the middle of the horse, and the audience gasped. The girl had designed some kind of pulley mechanism inside the belly of the horse to simulate the thrusting action of a man's erection while she rode the animal for everyone's amusement.

"Ingenious," Clover nodded, already beginning to feel her pussy watering at the prospect of watching the girl fucking herself while she rode the pony.

"Talk about hung like a *horse*," Jessop chuckled. "That poker must be at least a foot long. I can't imagine how she's going to get that whole thing inside her–"

"Maybe she *isn't*," Tara said, watching the girl starting to rotate the horse in a three-hundred-and-sixty-degree circle on the illuminated stage as she rocked it harder and harder.

With each tilting, the wooden dowel in the center of the horse rose higher and deeper over the arched saddle, teasing the audience with its anatomically correct shape and skin-colored pigmentation, making it look just like a man's erect penis.

"Fuck, that's hot," Clover panted, strumming her fingers over the base of her mound while she became progressively aroused watching the beginning of the girl's performance. "I wish *I* had a toy like that when I was growing up..."

"I wouldn't say it's exactly a *toy*," Tara laughed as she ran her eyes over the girl's sexy body. "And she certainly looks all grown up to me."

"Look," Jessop said, noticing the girl raising a small bucket from the side of the stage and pouring some shiny fluid over the top of the raised instrument as the liquid dribbled down the sides of its shaft. "Is that some kind of lubrication?"

"I would imagine so," the old lady said. "Some of our tribespeople use a mixture of natural aloe, shae butter, and jojoba oil to create their own personal lubricant. It's quite sensuous and slippery for the right applications–"

"I'd say this is the *perfect* application," Jessop grinned as his own prick began to harden, imagining it was his erection the girl was going to ride instead of the inanimate object on the horse.

The girl paused for a moment as she smiled at the audience, they she swung one leg over the hollowed-out saddle, sitting down slowly over the improvised dildo. She gripped the handmade, flowing mane of the horse, then started gently rocking the apparatus while she moaned softly and her eyes glazed over in pleasure.

"It's hard to see anything from this perspective," Jessop complained, twisting his body from side to side, trying to gain a better viewing angle of the girl rocking her hips over the pumping dildo.

"Give her a moment to get into the swing of things," Gisella smiled, noticing the position of the horse beginning to turn as the girl picked up her pace and leaned her body to one side.

"Yes, I see it now," Jessop nodded, flaring his eyes when

he saw the painted prick sliding in and out of her rising hips as the girl rocked it harder while the wooden horse turned its ass further in the direction of the crowd.

By the time she'd turned it a-hundred-and-eighty-degrees around, the group could clearly see her ass cheeks flexing and rising over the saddle as the pink dildo plowed ever deeper into her dripping folds.

"Fuck me," Tara gushed, ramming two fingers into her pussy while she watched the erotic performance, utterly transfixed like the rest of the groaning audience. "You were saying what you wanted to come back as in your second life–?"

"*Fuck* the ben-wa balls or the oversize cucumber," Clover panted, probing her own pussy next to the old lady. "In my next life, I want to come back as that horse."

"Do you want a little help with that?" Gisella said, rubbing her thigh against Clover's as they jilled themselves simultaneously, watching the girl pumping her hips over the bobbing pole on the horse's back.

"I think I'm going to need something a little bigger than my hands," Clover nodded, suddenly aware of the missing ladyboy cock when she needed it most.

"Something like *this*?" Gisella said, sliding her hand down to the side of her hips and raising a large, polished stump, carved in the shape of a man's erect penis.

"Yes, please," Clover nodded, grasping the improvised dildo eagerly when Gisella handed it to her and plowing it deeply into her dripping tunnel as she rammed it into her pussy with two hands.

"She looks like she's almost ready to get off," Tara panted, jilling her own pussy equally hard while she watched the flushed face of the moaning girl come back into view as she continued rocking the horse harder and swinging the upturned head of the pony back toward the front of the crowd. She began to lean forward, rocking the horse faster to drive its polished pecker deeper into her hole, then she swung her arms tightly around its neck and yawned her mouth open as she clung on the precipice of a powerful orgasm. When she finally uttered a deep, guttural growl, shaking uncontrollably over the rocking horse while she gripped its flanks in a vice-grip with her trembling legs, a loud moan began to spread around the perimeter of the amphitheater as the rest of the crowd soon reached the peak of their own pleasure, jerking and jilling their own bare private parts in turn.

After everybody finished groaning in one giant synchronized climax, there was a long silence in the stadium as the girl collapsed against the wooden horse's upturned neck while she savored the feeling of the slippery dick still embedded in her throbbing pussy. Then everyone slowly stood up from their seats, giving her the most rousing and passionate ovation of any performer so far.

"Yeah," Jessop nodded, holding his own spent tool in his two hands as he panted in satisfaction from one of the most stimulating sexual performances he'd ever witnessed.

"Do you think you'll be able to top that tomorrow night?" Gisella said, glancing at his throbbing dick spilling long streams of leftover cum down the edges of his deep-red-colored shaft.

"It's going to be hard," he said, smiling sheepishly back at her. "But I've got something quite different in mind..."

"Hard can be *good*," she smiled. "Especially when you're demonstrating it for the enjoyment of the rest of the community."

"I'm going to need a bit of time to rest and recover before I'm ready to go live," he panted.

"You've got twenty-four hours," the old lady said, glancing at his impressive instrument. "I'm looking forward to seeing what you come up with."

*R*eady for more erotic chills and thrills? Read the next volume in Clover's Fantasy Adventures: *Coming of Age, Part 2.* Buy direct and save at *victoriarusherotica.* Or download from your favorite online bookstore here: *retailer links.*

In the remote village of Whisperwood, there are a thousand ways to pleasure yourself...

ALSO BY VICTORIA RUSH

Adult Fairytales:

The Enchanted Forest: An Erotic Fairytale

The Land of Giants: An Erotic Fairytale

The Dragon's Lair: An Erotic Fairytale

Witch's Brew: An Erotic Fairytale

The Mage's Spell: An Erotic Fairytale

The Mermaid Lagoon: An Erotic Fairytale

The Coven: An Erotic Fairytale

Rapunzel: An Erotic Fairytale

The Seven Dwarfs: An Erotic Fairytale

The Land of Mutants: An Erotic Fairytale

The Erotic Temple: A Sexy Fairytale (Coming Soon)

Erotica Themed Bundles:

Voyeur: Lesbian Erotica Bundle

Public Affairs: A Lesbian Anthology

Futa Fantasies: The Ladyboy Collection

Threesomes: The Lesbian Collection

Threesomes - Volume 2: The Lesbian Collection

First Time: A Lesbian Anthology

Hedonism: An Erotic Anthology

Switch Hitters: Bisexual Erotica

Taboo Erotica: The Lesbian Series

BDSM: The Lesbian Collection

Party Games: The Erotic Collection

Party Games 2: The Erotic Collection

All Girl 1: Lesbian Erotica Bundle

All Girl 2: Lesbian Erotica Bundle

All Girl 3: Lesbian Erotica Bundle

All Girl 4: Lesbian Erotica Bundle

Erotic Fairytale Bundles:

Clover's Fantasy Adventures: Books 1 - 5

Clover's Fantasy Adventures: Books 6 - 10

Erotic Fantasy:

Pirate's Bounty: A Time Travel Adventure

Wild West: A Time Travel Adventure

Private Riley: A Time Travel Adventure

Cleopatra's Secret: A Time Travel Adventure

Bounty Hunter 2125: A Time Travel Adventure

Ninja Assassin: A Time Travel Adventure

The 300: A Time Travel Adventure

Arabian Nights: An Erotic Fairytale (coming soon...)

Steamy Time Travel Bundles:

Riley's Time Travel Adventures: Books 1 - 5

Lesbian Erotica:

The Dinner Party: Lesbian Voyeur Erotica

The Darkroom: Bisexual Voyeur Erotica

Naked Yoga: Lesbian Transgender Erotica

Nude Cruise: Bisexual Voyeur Erotica

Rush Hour: Taboo Public Sex

The Girl Next Door: First Time Lesbian Erotic Romance

Girls' Camp: Lesbian Group Sex

Wet Dream: Ladyboy Fantasy Erotica

The Convent: Taboo Sex with a Nun

Sex Robot: A Dream Sex Machine

The Personal Trainer: Getting Pumped at the Gym

The Dominatrix: BDSM Lesbian Domination

Webcam Chat: Lesbian Online Sex

Paint Me: A Kinky Bodypainting Workshop

The Toy Party: Girls Sharing Sex Toys

The Costume Party: Strapping One On

Swedish Sauna: Lesbian Group Sex

The Therapist: Taboo Lesbian Erotica

Elevator Shaft: Bisexual Threesomes Erotica

Ladyboy: Lesbian Transgender Erotica

Peep Show: Lesbian Voyeur Erotica

The Dare: Public Sex Erotica

Maid Service: Lesbian Threesomes Erotica

The Hitchhiker: First Time Lesbian Erotica

The Housesitter: Spycam Lesbian Erotica

The Spa: Lesbian Group Orgy

Parlor Games: Blindfold Sex Party

The Exchange Student: First Time Lesbian Erotica

The Hostel: Bisexual Group Erotica

The Harem: Lesbian Erotic Romance

The Orient Express: Lesbian Voyeur Erotica

The First Lady: A Forbidden Lesbian Erotic Romance

The Slave: Lesbian BDSM Erotica

The Masseuse: Lesbian Sensuous Erotica

Too Close for Comfort: Lesbian Forbidden Erotica

Naked Twister: A Wild Party Game

Lexi: The Sex App (Lesbian Fantasy Erotica)

Call Girl: Lesbian Bisexual Threesomes Erotica

Circle Jill: Lesbian Masturbation Workshop

The Viewing Room: Masturbation Voyeur Erotica

Spin the Bottle: A Kinky Party Game

The Hair Salon: Lesbian Voyeur Erotica

Tribadism 1: Girls Only Sex Workshop

Tribadism 2: The Art of Scissoring

Tribadism 3: Threeway Hookups

The Kiss: A Game of Oral Sex

Pledge Week: Sorority Sisters

Carny Games 1: A Wild Sex Party

Carny Games 2: A Kinky Sex Party

Carny Games 3: An Erotic Sex Party

Dreamscape: An Artificial Reality Game

Glory Hole: Guess Who's On the Other Side

Joy Ride: A Late Night Erotic Bus Trip

The Blind Girl: An Erotic Romance(Coming Soon)

Lesbian Erotica Bundles:

Jade's Erotic Adventures: Books 1 - 5

Jade's Erotic Adventures: Books 6 - 10

Jade's Erotic Adventures: Books 11 - 15

Jade's Erotic Adventures: Books 16 - 20

Jade's Erotic Adventures: Books 21 - 25

Jade's Erotic Adventures: Books 26 - 30

Jade's Erotic Adventures: Books 31 - 35

Jade's Erotic Adventures: Books 36 - 40

Jade's Erotic Adventures: Books 41 - 45

Jade's Erotic Adventures: Books 46 - 50

Fifty Shades of Jade: Superbundle

Standalone Stories:

The Polynesian Girl: A Lesbian EroticRomance